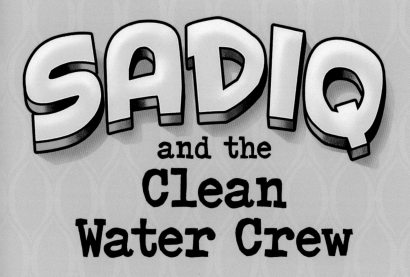

SADIQ

and the
Clean
Water Crew

BY SIMAN NUURALI

ART BY CHRISTOS SKALTSAS

PICTURE WINDOW BOOKS
a capstone imprint

Published by Picture Window Books, an imprint of Capstone.
1710 Roe Crest Drive
North Mankato, Minnesota 56003
capstonepub.com

Library of Congress Cataloging-in-Publication Data:
Names: Nuurali, Siman, author. | Skaltsas, Christos, illustrator.
Title: Sadiq and the Clean Water Crew / by Siman Nuurali ; art by Christos
Skaltsas.
Description: North Mankato, Minnesota : Picture Window Books, an
imprint of Capstone, [2022] | Series: Sadiq | Audience: Ages 6-8. |
Audience: Grades 2-3. | Summary: Sadiq's class is visiting the pond on a
nature field trip, but the dead fish they find there is disturbing; when he
finds that the likely cause is pollution, he and a group of his classmates
form the Clean Water Crew to do what they can to help clean up not just
their pond, but other bodies of water as well.
Identifiers: LCCN 2021033289 (print) | LCCN 2021033290 (ebook) | ISBN
9781663977120 (hardcover) | ISBN 9781666330724 (paperback) | ISBN
9781666330731 (pdf)
Subjects: LCSH: Somali Americans—Juvenile fiction. | Children of
immigrants—Juvenile fiction. | Water—Pollution—Juvenile fiction. |
Nature conservation—Juvenile fiction. | Helping behavior—Juvenile
fiction. | CYAC: Somali Americans—Fiction. | Immigrants—Fiction. |
Water—Pollution—Fiction. | Ponds—Fiction. | Wildlife conservation—
Fiction. | Clubs—Fiction.
Classification: LCC PZ7.1.N9 Sacm 2022 (print) | LCC PZ7.1.N9 (ebook) |
DDC [Fic]—dc23
LC record available at https://lccn.loc.gov/2021033289
LC ebook record available at https://lccn.loc.gov/2021033290

Designer: Tracy Davies

Design Elements: Shutterstock/Irtsya

Printed and bound in the USA.   4608

TABLE OF CONTENTS

FACTS ABOUT SOMALIA

- Somali people come from many different clans.

- Many Somalis are nomadic. That means they travel from place to place. They search for water, food, and land for their animals.

- Somalia is mostly desert. It doesn't rain often there.

- The camel is an important animal to Somali people. Camels can survive a long time without food or water.

- Around ninety-nine percent of all Somalis are Muslim.

SOMALI TERMS

baba (BAH-baah)—a common word for father

hooyo (HOY-yoh)—mother

qalbi (KUHL-bee)—my heart

salaam (sa-LAHM)—a short form of Arabic greeting, used by many Muslims. It also means "peace."

wiilkeyga (wil-KAY-gaah)—my son

CHAPTER 1

TURTLE FRIENDS

"Guess what's happening tomorrow?" said Sadiq. He plopped down on Aliya's bed.

"I won't guess if you don't get off my bed," said his sister, grinning. She shoved Sadiq's shoulder playfully.

"Oh c'mon, take a guess," said Sadiq. "If you do, I promise I will get up."

"Okay, fine," said Aliya. She tilted her head. "Let me think. . . ."

"Today?" teased Sadiq. He pointed at his watch.

"You'll become funny tomorrow?" said Aliya, laughing.

"Ha ha, Aliya," said Sadiq with a smile. "No. We're going on a field trip! Are you jealous?"

"That sounds fun, so yes I am!" said Aliya. "Where are you going?"

"To a park that has a big pond," replied Sadiq. "Ms. Battersby said it's got fish and frogs and all kinds of stuff."

"Ew, frogs!" said Aliya, crinkling her nose. "They're slimy. Bleh!"

"Maybe I'll get one for you, then," said Sadiq. "Ribbit!"

"Don't you dare!" Aliya said. She tossed a pillow at her brother. "I do love turtles, though!"

"Everyone knows that!" said Sadiq. Aliya's walls were covered with pictures of turtles, and she had a stuffed turtle on her bed. They were her favorite animal!

"Did you know turtles are reptiles?" asked Aliya. "They spend most of their time in water."

"I know they can live on land sometimes too, right?" replied Sadiq.

"Correct!" said Aliya, smiling. "And did you know they've been around a loooooong time? Like, hundreds of millions of years!"

"What?" said Sadiq, his eyes widening. "That can't be true!"

"It is," said Aliya, nodding. "Ask *Hooyo* if you like. She'll tell you the same thing."

"Ms. Battersby said we should research one animal," said Sadiq. "Maybe I should look up turtles. They sound amazing!"

"They are!" Aliya agreed. "I hope you see one tomorrow."

"I hope so too," said Sadiq. "Do you think it will be a sea turtle?"

"No," replied Aliya, shaking her head. "They are only found in the sea. That's why they're called *sea* turtles!"

"Well, a *pond* turtle then," said Sadiq. "I'm going to see if Hooyo can help me research."

"Say hello for me!" said Aliya.

"To Hooyo?" Sadiq asked as he was leaving Aliya's room.

"No, you silly goose," said Aliya. "To my turtle friends at the pond!"

"I will!" said Sadiq.

Sadiq ran downstairs and bounded into the kitchen, where Hooyo was working at her laptop.

"Whoa there!" said Hooyo, holding up a hand. "Slow down, speedster. You know you're not to run in the house."

"I'm sorry, Hooyo," said Sadiq as he sat down. "I wanted to talk to you."

"What about, *qalbi*?" asked Hooyo. "Is everything okay?"

"Yes, Hooyo, I'm fine," replied Sadiq. "Tomorrow's our field trip."

"To the park?" asked Hooyo. "Did I forget to sign your slip?"

"No, it's signed," said Sadiq. "But I need help researching an animal."

"Sure thing," said Hooyo. "What animal?"

"Aliya told me some cool things about turtles," said Sadiq. "So I picked them."

"Oh! I thought maybe you picked cheetahs, because of how fast you ran into the kitchen!" Hooyo joked.

"Hooyo!" Sadiq said and laughed.

"No cheetahs live at the pond—I hope!"

Hooyo laughed too. "You are right about that," she said. "I just sent my last email, so we can start now, if you'd like."

"Great!" said Sadiq. "Thanks, Hooyo!"

Hooyo and Sadiq went online and looked up turtles.

"What does en . . . dan . . . jer . . ." Sadiq sounded out a word. "I can't say that word, Hooyo. What does it mean?"

"Endangered," said Hooyo. "It means at risk of becoming extinct. The word *extinct* means to disappear."

"Disappear?" said Sadiq, frowning.

"Like in magic tricks?"

"No, qalbi," said Hooyo. "It means all the animals of that kind die. None are left."

"So, there won't be any more turtles ever?" asked Sadiq sadly.

"None of those kind. If we don't protect them," replied Hooyo. "We have to take steps to keep them safe."

"How can we do that?" asked Sadiq. He looked up at his mother.

"To begin with, people can stop throwing plastic in the ocean," said Hooyo. "Turtles and other animals get trapped in it or eat it, and they sometimes die."

"I don't know how to help," said Sadiq, looking down.

"Learning about the problem is a good start," said Hooyo.

Sadiq and Hooyo spent the next hour learning about sea turtles and looking for ways to help.

CHAPTER 2

The next morning, Hooyo drove Sadiq to school. Sadiq had his reusable water bottle and his sack lunch. He was ready for the field trip!

"There's Zaza and Manny!" said Sadiq when they pulled up to the school. "And the bus for the field trip is already here. Bye, Hooyo! Thank you!"

"Have fun at the park!" Hooyo called after him. "Watch out for cheetahs!"

Sadiq laughed and waved goodbye to her.

"Hi, Zaza! Hi, Manny!" he said when he caught up with his friends.

"Hi, Sadiq!" the boys replied. They climbed onto the bus and found seats together.

"Okay, third graders!" said Ms. Battersby, clapping her hands. "Settle down so we can leave."

The school bus pulled out of the lot and headed to the park.

"I can't wait to splash around," said a boy named Auggie. He was a playful kid in Sadiq's class.

"I want to skip rocks on the water," said a boy named Carter.

"You'll have to teach me how to do that," said Sadiq.

Sadiq discovered that all the kids were excited, but for different reasons.

"Splashing and skipping rocks will be fun. But I really hope we see some fish and turtles," said Sadiq. *Then I can tell Aliya I met her friends!* he thought to himself and giggled.

***

"We're here!" Ms. Battersby announced when they arrived at the park.

Everyone got off the bus and gathered around the teacher. She went over the safety rules for the day. Then she said, "It's time to explore!

Remember to take notes about the animals you see."

She held up a stack of cards. "I printed out bingo cards," she said and began handing them out. "Check off each animal, insect, or bird you see."

Sadiq looked at his card.

butterfly	slug	water strider	leech	minnows
toad	fish	other bird	turtle	worm
snake	dragonfly	FREE SPACE	spider	heron
other insect	snail	beetle	frog	mosquito
gret	fly	tadpole	mussels	duck

"After you get a bingo, your prize is to play games in the park!" said Ms. Battersby.

"Hooray!" cheered the kids. They took off running toward the pond with their bingo cards.

"I think I already see a duck!" Manny called out.

"Quack!" said Auggie, and he started to waddle.

The kids marked an X over "duck" on their cards.

"Look, a crow!" said Zaza, pointing.

"Where?" asked Sadiq. "Oh, I see it on that branch. Good eyes, Zaza!"

Sadiq high-fived Zaza. They checked "other bird" off on their cards.

The kids walked slowly through the tall grasses around the pond, checking animals off their cards as they went.

"Look!" said Carter, getting down on his knees. "It's a dragonfly!"

"Oh, wow! It's got cool blue wings," said Manny. "Let's check it off!"

"Bingo!" said Zaza. "I got a whole row of animals! I'm going over to the playground," he said. "Last one there is a turtle!"

Zaza took off running, followed by Manny and Auggie. Other kids who had their bingos ran after them too.

"I think I'll keep looking for animals by the pond," said Sadiq.

"I'll come with you," said Carter.

"Okay!" said Sadiq, smiling. "Maybe you can show me how to skip rocks."

Sadiq and Carter continued their way around the pond while chatting. Sadiq was telling his friend how long turtles have been around.

"No way!" said Carter, his eyes widening. "Hundreds of millions of years?"

"Yes, way!" said Sadiq. "My sister Aliya told me."

The boys moved carefully through the tall grass to get a little closer to the water. Ms. Battersby had told them it was important not to disturb the wildlife.

"Oh look, Sadiq," said Carter, pointing to the water. "There's a few silver fishes here."

"Bingo!" said Sadiq quietly, so as not to bother the animals.

"I think I see tadpoles too," said Sadiq. "They'll become frogs when they get bigger. My sister does *not* like frogs."

"My mom doesn't either!" said Carter.

They moved along the bank of the pond looking for more animals.

"Oh, I think I see a turtle!" called out Sadiq.

"Where?" said Carter, hurrying to catch up.

"Right there," said Sadiq, pointing.

"He's sunning himself on that rock in the water."

"Oh, I see it!" said Carter.

"Aliya says hi!" Sadiq called out to the turtle. He was so happy to check "turtle" off his bingo card!

"What's that weird stuff at the edge of the water?" asked Carter. "It looks like slime."

"Let me see," said Sadiq, leaning closer. "It looks like some type of fish."

"They're not moving though," said Carter.

Sadiq sniffed the air. There was a faint rotten smell. "I think it's fish, but they're dead," said Sadiq, sadly. "Look, there's at least four of them."

"What do you think happened?"
asked Carter.

"I don't know. We could ask Ms.
Battersby," Sadiq suggested.

The boys walked toward Ms.
Battersby. She was taking the students'
lunch sacks out of the cooler.

"What did you boys discover?" she asked Sadiq and Carter.

"Dead fish," said Sadiq. "We don't know what happened to them. We wanted to ask you."

"That happens sometimes," said Ms. Battersby. "Fish die of natural causes. But if you see a group of dead fish, it might be a clue that something else killed them."

Sadiq and Carter looked at each other. They both frowned.

Then Carter said, "Want me to teach you to skip rocks?"

"Race you back to the pond!" Sadiq replied.

CHAPTER 3

BACK TO THE POND

"How was your field trip, *wiilkeyga*?" asked *Baba* the next morning in the kitchen. "Did you see a lot of cool animals?"

"It was great, Baba!" said Sadiq. "I had the best time! Carter and I saw a turtle."

"You did? Did you say hello for me?" asked Aliya, excitedly.

"I did! But it must have been sleeping, because it didn't answer," Sadiq teased.

"What else did you see?" asked Nuurali.

"Well, we saw some fish," replied Sadiq. "But some of them were dead. Our teacher said that happens sometimes."

"That's true, qalbi," said Hooyo. "All animals eventually die."

"That's what Ms. Battersby said," said Sadiq, nodding. "But this was a group of dead fish. They were covered with slimy stuff."

"It's possible the water wasn't safe for them," said Baba. "Something not healthy in it."

"Like what, Baba?" asked Sadiq, turning to his dad.

"Sometimes chemicals get dumped in the water," replied Baba. "It can poison the wildlife."

"Can we drive there so I can show you?" Sadiq asked. "I think Carter might want to come too. He was with me when we found them."

"Yes, qalbi," said Baba. "Why don't you go and call him. Have him ask his parents for permission."

Sadiq left the table to call his friend. Soon he ran back into the kitchen. "Carter said he can come!" said Sadiq.

"I guess *I* am going on a field trip today!" said Baba, smiling at Hooyo.

In the car, Sadiq and Carter told Baba more about what they'd seen at the park.

"Was it scary to see the dead fish?" Baba asked the boys.

"It wasn't scary," replied Carter. "But it made me sad to see them like that."

"I am sure that was hard," said Baba, nodding.

Soon they were at the park. The boys got out of the car, and Sadiq took his dad's hand.

"This way, Baba!" he said, tugging.

"Slow down, Sadiq!" said Baba, laughing. "We'll get there soon enough."

"Look, Sadiq!" said Carter when they got to the pond. "The fish are still there. I thought they might have floated away."

"I see the slime you mentioned, Sadiq," said Baba. He squatted to take a closer look. "I think I was right about the water being unsafe."

"Baba, do you think they were sick?" asked Sadiq. "I didn't know fish could get sick."

"Yes, they were sick, qalbi," replied Baba. "Something in the water made them sick."

"Can we find out what it was, Mr. Mohamed?" asked Carter. "Maybe we can save the other fish."

Baba shook his head. "The water would have to be collected in samples. Then sent in for testing by scientists at a lab."

"Oh, that's too bad," said Carter. "I wanted to help them."

"Hmm," said Baba. "Learning more is a way to help. Who would like to go to the aquarium?"

"ME!" Sadiq and Carter shouted at once. It was just what the boys needed to cheer them up.

***

When Baba and the boys got to the aquarium, there weren't too many visitors. Baba said his friend worked there and might show them around.

"*Salaam*!" said Baba. "Dr. Carroll, meet Sadiq and Carter." Baba told the boys, "Dr. Carroll is a scientist, and a friend of mine from college."

"Hi, boys," said Dr. Carroll, smiling. "You can call me Bobbie. Mr. Mohamed tells me you have some questions."

"Hi, Bobbie," said the boys shyly. They were nervous about asking a real scientist questions!

"Do you make fish better?" asked Sadiq. "We found fish that were sick and died. Are you that kind of doctor?"

"Kind of," replied Bobbie with a smile. "I am a zoologist. Do you know what that is?"

Sadiq and Carter shook their heads.

"A zoologist is someone who studies animal life," explained Bobbie. "I help take care of the fish and turtles here. I also study them and educate others about them."

"That's really cool, Bobbie!" said Carter. "Mr. Mohamed said you might know why the fish died."

"Sometimes chemicals can get into the water," said Bobbie. "Some chemicals make the water unsafe for animals. That causes the animals to get sick and die."

"That's really sad," said Carter. "Can we stop it?"

"Yes, Carter," said Bobbie. "We can all do our part to keep the ponds safe.

Businesses, communities, and people must all work together to help keep our waterways clean."

"I learned that sea turtles aren't safe either," said Sadiq.

Bobbie nodded. "That is true. Ocean animals have similar problems. Whether in a small pond or in the big ocean, all animals need clean water to survive."

Bobbie thought for a moment. Then she said, "I have some booklets for you." She led the boys over to a table. "There are some things you can do to help."

The boys flipped through the pages and read a few tips:

- Pick up pet waste and put it in the garbage. Otherwise waste can end up in drains and wash into ponds and lakes. The bacteria in the waste can make animals sick.

- Wash vehicles on the lawn, not on the driveway. If the soapy water gets into a storm drain, it can harm neighborhood ponds.

- Keep things clean. Sweep grass clippings off the driveway, sidewalk, and street, and then compost them. Clean any spilled oil or chemicals like bleach and don't let them go down the drain.

"Now, since you mentioned sea turtles, would you like to meet ours?" Bobbie asked.

"Yes!" the boys both said. They headed over to ocean animals exhibit.

Sadiq couldn't wait to tell Aliya all about it.

CHAPTER 4

WHAT CAN WE DO?

The next Monday, the kids were back in science class.

"Did everyone have fun on the field trip?" asked Ms. Battersby. "I saw all your completed bingo cards. Well done, third graders!"

"I saw squishy slugs!" said Auggie, smiling. "They looked gross, so I didn't pick them up."

"I saw a bald eagle!" said Zaza.

"That's great, Zaza!" said Ms. Battersby.

"Bald eagles used to be endangered. The government made rules about protecting them. Now their numbers are growing in the wild!"

"My mom said some turtles are endangered," said Sadiq. "Carter and I saw fish that died in the pond. I am worried they might become endangered too."

"There is a small pond by my house," said Suaad. "Now it's covered in something called algae. My mom says that's a sign it might be polluted."

"I saw that on a lake my dad took me to," said Zaza. "We were going to go fishing. But we couldn't because of the algae."

"We should try to help!" Sadiq said to Ms. Battersby. "Maybe we can do something to keep the ponds clean."

"That sounds like a good idea, Sadiq," replied Ms. Battersby. She looked at the clock. "But class is over. We'll talk more about it another time."

After school, Sadiq, Zaza, and Manny walked home together.

"I really wish we could help," said Sadiq. "The fish and turtles need us."

"But what can we do about it? We're just kids," said Zaza.

"Baba took Carter and me to the aquarium," said Sadiq. "We met a zoologist named Dr. Carroll. She was really cool and had ideas of how to help."

"Things we can do?" asked Zaza, excitedly.

"I think so," said Sadiq, thoughtfully. "She gave me a booklet with some ideas."

"Can I see?" asked Manny.

"Sure," replied Sadiq. "It's right here in my backpack." Sadiq stopped to take it out.

Manny flipped it open. "It says to give your business to companies that don't pollute the environment. And here it says to vote for lawmakers who will make laws protecting nature," said Manny.

"But we're kids! We can't do that stuff," said Zaza.

"That's true," said Manny. "But kids can do stuff too. Here it says to wash cars on the lawn, not the driveway. I help my dad wash the car. Next time, we'll do it on the grass!"

"Yes!" said Sadiq, smiling. "There's a lot that kids can do! We should start a club!"

"Okay! What should we call it?" asked Manny.

"Clean Club?" said Zaza.

"That's a cool name," said Manny. "But we are helping keep ponds clean. It should say something about water."

"How about the Clean Water Crew?" suggested Sadiq. "That way people will know what we do."

"Perfect!" said Zaza.

"I hope we can get kids to join," said Manny.

"I think we can," said Sadiq. "I know for sure Carter will."

"I think Suaad will too," said Zaza. "She was worried about the pond near her house."

"Hooray for the Clean Water Crew!" cheered Manny.

CHAPTER 5

HELP IS ON THE WAY!

Sadiq went to school early the next day. He wanted to speak to Ms. Battersby about their club.

"Hello, Ms. Battersby!" said Sadiq.

"Good morning, Sadiq," she replied. "You're early. Is everything okay?"

"Everything is great," said Sadiq. "I just wanted to tell you about our club."

"A new club?" asked Ms. Battersby. "I think I know what it might be. Can I guess?"

"Yes!" said Sadiq, grinning. "You might get it right."

"Did you find a way to help the fish?" she asked.

"I hope so!" said Sadiq. "We thought we could help by changing some of the things we do. This booklet from the aquarium has a lot of ideas."

"I like your thinking, Sadiq," said Ms. Battersby. "What's the name of the club?"

"The Clean Water Crew," said Sadiq. "Do you like it?"

"I love it," said Ms. Battersby. "How can I help?"

***

The next day after school, ten students gathered in the gym for the first Clean Water Crew meeting. Sadiq was very excited!

"Look how many kids showed up!" said Sadiq. "I was worried no one would want to help *clean*."

"We all want to help, Sadiq" said Carter. "Thank you for asking me to join. How do we get started?"

"Ms. Battersby is going to take notes on the whiteboard. We're going to come up with a list of ideas from the internet," said Sadiq.

"And we can add some from this," said Carter, holding up his booklet from Dr. Carroll.

The students began calling out ideas. Some had checked out library books. Others looked on the internet.

"A tip in the booklet says to use rain barrels instead of letting rain from your spouts run into the streets," said Carter.

"It says here to pick weeds by hand instead of using chemicals to kill them," Suaad read from the internet.

"And to help the oceans, we should avoid plastics that can only be used one time," said Sadiq. "My hooyo told me that one!"

Soon Ms. Battersby had written a long list of ideas from the students on the whiteboard.

"There's a lot of stuff on this list we can do," said Manny.

"Yes, but how do we get people to do it?" asked Zaza.

The kids were quiet for a while, thinking.

Suddenly, Sadiq said, "Bingo!"

"Bingo?" asked Carter.

"The bingo cards! We can make some like Ms. Battersby did for our field trip!"

"Great idea!" We can write one idea in each box," said Carter. "And people can check them off as they do them. Like we checked off the animals we saw!"

"That's awesome!" said Zaza. "I think it will work!"

The kids got busy making the bingo cards. They decorated the cards with drawings of all kinds of water animals. Sadiq drew sea turtles on his.

"Should we have a prize?" asked Suaad. "For when people get a bingo?"

"Good idea," said Ms. Battersby, nodding. "It might make everyone try harder."

"Everyone likes pizza!" said Sadiq. "Can we have a pizza party for the bingo winners?"

"I think that could be arranged," said Ms. Battersby.

"Thank you, Ms. Battersby!" said Sadiq.

"Okay, kids, let's go to the office to make copies of the bingo cards for all the students who want to participate," said Ms. Battersby.

"We could put the extras in the media center—so that the whole school can help if they want!" Carter said.

The students walked with Ms. Battersby to the office.

"I can't wait for the pizza party," said Zaza. "I am going to try to win!"

"Pizza is great, Zaza," said Sadiq. "But the fish and turtles will get the real prize—a cleaner, safer home!"

Sadiq and Carter smiled and gave each other a high five.

GLOSSARY

algae (AL-jee)—small plants without roots or stems that grow in water

aquarium (uh-KWAYR-ee-uhm)—a glass tank where pets, such as hamsters, hermit crabs, or fish, are kept

chemical (KEH-muh-kuhl)—a substance used in or produced by chemistry; medicines, gunpowder, and food preservatives all are made from chemicals

disturb (dih-STURB)—to bother or annoy

endangered (en-DAYN-juhrd)—in danger of dying out

eventually (e-VEN-chu-lee)—at some later time

exhibit (eg-ZIH-buht)—a display that shows off something to the public

extinct (ek-STINGKT)—no longer living; an extinct animal is one that has died out, with no more of its kind

jealous (JEL-uhss)—wanting something someone else has

lawmaker (LAW-MAY-kur)—an elected official who makes laws

polluted (puh-LOOT-ted)—unfit or harmful to living things

rain barrel (RAYN BA-ruhl)—a barrel that collects rainwater

similar (SIM-uh-ler)—almost the same as something else

zoologist (zoo-OLL-uh-gist)—a person who studies animals

TALK ABOUT IT

1. Think about the teamwork that was involved in getting the Clean Water Crew started. Sadiq and Carter asked adults for help and also came up with their own ideas. Name three people from the story who contributed and what they did to help.

2. How would the story be different if Sadiq and Carter had not stayed behind the other students and found the dead fish? Talk with a friend about what might have happened instead.

WRITE IT DOWN

1. Sadiq likes to start clubs to get friends together for a common cause or interest. Write a list of things a group can do that might be hard for one person to do alone. Are there things that might be easier for just one person to do? If so, make a list of those too.

2. Imagine you are Sadiq making an announcement at school about the Clean Water Club. Write down what you would say, including details about the club. Then practice saying it out loud.

ANIMAL BINGO!

Learning about animals is a good way to help them. Follow Sadiq's lead and make bingo cards for you, your family, and friends. Players will look up information about animals on their card. After they research an animal, they should share a fact with you about the animal, then put an X over that animal on their card. When someone gets a bingo by marking off any row— down, across, or diagonal—award them a prize!

WHAT YOU NEED:

- large sheets of construction paper
- pens or pencils
- a ruler
- scissors
- small candies or stickers

WHAT YOU DO:

1. Using the ruler, draw a 10 by 10 inch square on each paper. Cut it out. Each paper will make one bingo card.

2. Make 25 boxes in the square. Make five rows of five boxes each. Each box should be 2 by 2 inches. (Repeat for each bingo card you make.)

3. In each box, write the name of a different animal.

4. When someone gets a bingo, award them with a prize such as a homemade blue ribbon, a piece of candy, or animal stickers!

butterfly	slug	water strider	leech	minnows
toad	fish	other bird	turtle	worm
snake	dragonfly	FREE SPACE	spider	heron
other insect	snail	beetle	frog	mosquito
egret	fly	tadpole	mussels	duck

CREATORS

Siman Nuurali grew up in Kenya. She now lives in Minnesota. Siman and her family are Somali— just like Sadiq and his family! She and her five children love to play badminton and board games together. Siman works at Children's Hospital and, in her free time, she enjoys writing and reading.

Christos Skaltsas was born and raised in Athens, Greece. For the past fifteen years, he has worked as a freelance illustrator for children's book publishers. In his free time, he loves playing with his son, collecting vinyl records, and traveling around the world.